Did somebody say
INVENTION?!

D0999042

PRAISE FOR
THE INVENTION HUNTERS SERIES

"The text and illustrations succeed in grabbing the readers' attention because of the vivid colors and spirit of fun. The characters are quirky and silly, making this nonfiction book about simple machines…engaging."
—*School Library Connection*

"The balance of the fantastical story with scientific and historical facts makes this a good title to recommend to fiction and nonfiction readers alike."
—*School Library Journal*

"Engineering and comics for the youngest of readers."
—*A Fuse #8 Production*

Thanks to Dad, Mom,
and Kirsten

ABOUT THIS BOOK • The illustrations for this book were rendered digitally. • This book was edited by Andrea Spooner and designed by Karina Granda. The production was supervised by Virginia Lawther, and the production editor was Marisa Finkelstein. The text was set in Avenir LT Pro and Invention Hunters, and the display type is LunchBox and Rockwell.
• Copyright © 2019 by Korwin Briggs • Cover illustration copyright © 2019 by Korwin Briggs. Cover design by Karina Granda. Cover copyright © 2019 by Hachette Book Group, Inc. • Hachette Book Group supports the right to free expression and the value of copyright. The purpose of copyright is to encourage writers and artists to produce the creative works that enrich our culture. • The scanning, uploading, and distribution of this book without permission is a theft of the author's intellectual property. If you would like permission to use material from the book (other than for review purposes), please contact permissions@hbgusa.com. Thank you for your support of the author's rights.
• Little, Brown and Company • Hachette Book Group • 1290 Avenue of the Americas, New York, NY 10104 • Visit us at LBYR.com • Originally published in hardcover by Little, Brown and Company in July 2019 • First Trade Paperback Edition: July 2021 • Little, Brown and Company is a division of Hachette Book Group, Inc. The Little, Brown name and logo are trademarks of Hachette Book Group, Inc. • The publisher is not responsible for websites (or their content) that are not owned by the publisher. • The Library of Congress has cataloged the hardcover edition as follows: Names: Briggs, Korwin, author, illustrator. • Title: The Invention Hunters discover how machines work / written and illustrated by Korwin Briggs. • Description: First edition. | New York ; Boston : Little, Brown and Company, 2019. | Series: The Invention Hunters ; 1 | Summary: "When the Invention Hunters, a group of globe-trotting invention collectors, visit a construction site in their flying museum, a boy helps them by explaining how simple machines like levers, pulleys, and cranks work" —Provided by publisher. • Identifiers: LCCN 2017056650 | ISBN 9780316436793 (hardcover) | ISBN 9780316436786 (ebook) | ISBN 9780316436816 (library edition ebook) Subjects: | CYAC: Tools—Fiction. | Inventions—Fiction. • Classification: LCC PZ7.1.B7546 Inv 2019 | DDC [E]—dc23 • LC record available at https://lccn.loc.gov/2017056650 • ISBNs: 978-0-316-43683-0 (pbk.), 978-0-316-43677-9 (ebook), 978-0-316-43678-6 (ebook), 978-0-316-43682-3 (ebook) • PRINTED IN CHINA • 1010 • 10 9 8 7 6 5 4 3 2 1

THE INVENTION HUNTERS

DISCOVER HOW MACHINES WORK

 LITTLE, BROWN AND COMPANY
NEW YORK BOSTON

Written and illustrated by
KORWIN BRIGGS

IT'S A WHEELBARROW!

IT HELPS YOU LIFT AND MOVE THINGS!

When you use a wheelbarrow, you only have to lift one side of a heavy load. The other side rolls along smoothly on a wheel. A wheelbarrow is a kind of **LEVER!**

WHY DO THINGS MOVE?

When something moves, it's because a **FORCE** is pushing or pulling it. A force is anything that pushes or pulls on something. When you move a toy car, or kick a ball, or pull on a dog's leash, you're adding a force. The heavier something is, the more force it takes to move. That's why the Invention Hunters' museum needs so many rockets, propellers, and balloons—they all add the force it needs to fly!

HANDLE　　LOAD　　WHEEL

WHAT'S A LEVER?

A lever increases the force (or distance) of your push or pull. All levers have three things: a place to put your **LOAD**, a place (like a handle) where you apply **EFFORT**, and a **FULCRUM** (or turning point), like the wheel of a wheelbarrow. There are three kinds of levers:

A lever can be like a seesaw, where the fulcrum is between the effort and the load. When you push the handle down, the load goes up! **The longer the end with the handle is, the more you can lift.**

A lever can be like a wheelbarrow, where the load is between the effort and the fulcrum. When you lift the handle up, the load also moves! **The closer the load is to the fulcrum, the easier it is to lift.**

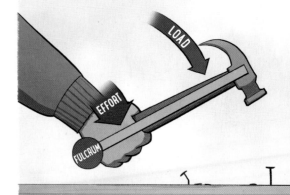

A lever can be like a hammer, where the effort is between the load and the fulcrum. When you move the handle a little, the load moves a lot! **The farther the load is from the handle, the more it moves.**

THE FIRST WHEELBARROWS were invented in China almost 2,000 years ago. They had one big wheel in the middle and space to carry things on either side. They might look different from wheelbarrows today, but they worked even better!

OUT OF THIS WORLD!

An ancient scientist named Archimedes once claimed that if he had a long enough lever and a place to stand, he could move the whole world!

IT'S A JACKHAMMER!

IT'S FOR BREAKING STUFF!

Inside a jackhammer, a heavy **HAMMER** hits a pointed **WEDGE**. Air blows in from one direction and pushes the hammer up. Then air comes from a different direction and blows the hammer down into the wedge. As the hammer bangs the wedge into the ground again and again, it cracks the surface apart!

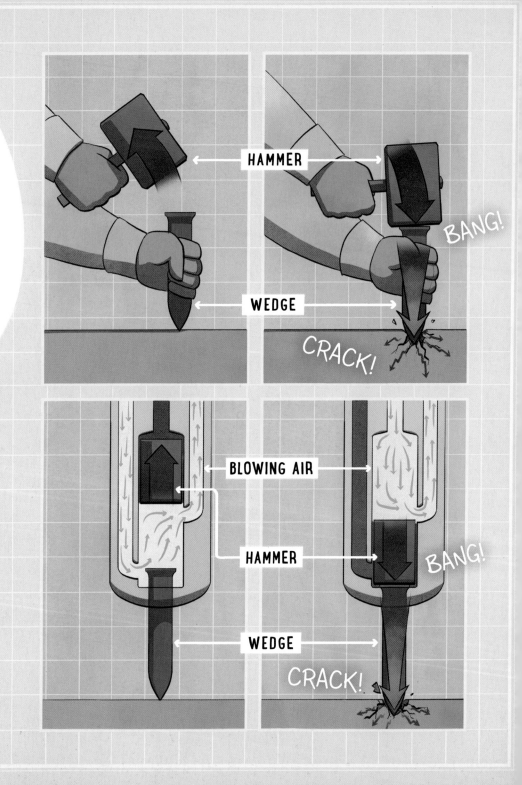

HAMMER

WEDGE

BANG!

CRACK!

BLOWING AIR

HAMMER

WEDGE

BANG!

CRACK!

STONE HAND AX

1,700,000s BCE

One of the world's first tools was a rock wedge called a **HAND AX**, which people made by breaking off chunks of rocks. They may have used them to cut meat, plants, animal skins, and wood.

BRONZE CHISEL

2600s BCE

About 6,500 years ago, people learned to melt copper and other metals together to make **BRONZE**. Using a hammer and a bronze wedge called a **CHISEL**, people could cut rocks quickly and precisely.

IRON PICK

1500-1000 BCE

Hundreds of years later, people learned to use **IRON**, a metal stronger than bronze. One tool they made was a **PICK**: a chisel attached to a stick, so you could swing it like a hammer.

JACKHAMMER

1850s CE

The **WEDGE** in a jackhammer is made of a tough metal called **STEEL**. Steel was invented more than 3,000 years ago, but back then it was very rare and expensive. Now we're much better at making it. We use steel in tools, buildings, cars, planes, and much more!

BEAK HAMMER!

A jackhammer's wedge can hit the ground up to 25 times every second. That's even faster than a woodpecker pecks!

IT'S A CRANE!

IT'S FOR LIFTING THINGS!

A CRANE is made of two smaller machines: a PULLEY and a CRANK. A ROPE (or another kind of line) is connected to the crank and then hung over the pulley. When the crank turns, it pulls one end of the rope down from the pulley. And that pulls the other end of the rope up!

WHAT'S A PULLEY?

A pulley is a wheel with a groove on its edge that a rope or chain fits into.

When you pull one end down, the other end goes up!

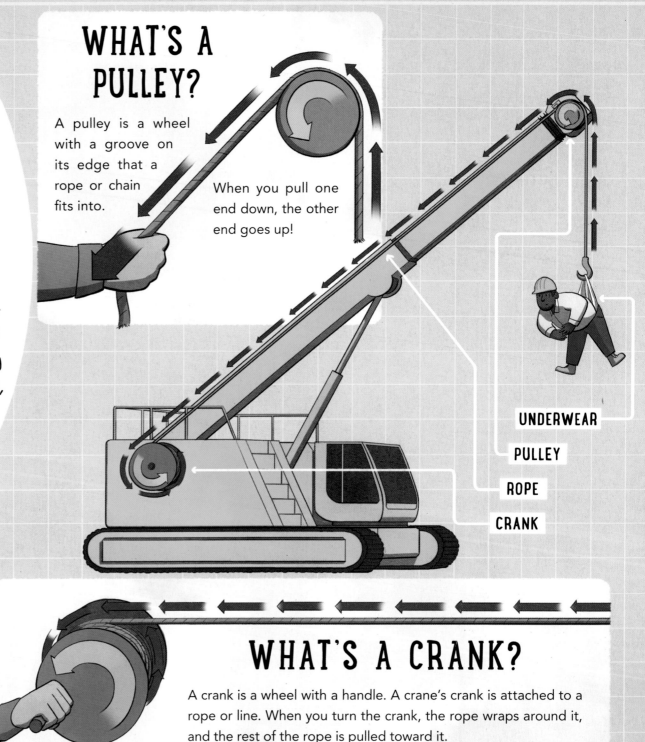

UNDERWEAR

PULLEY

ROPE

CRANK

WHAT'S A CRANK?

A crank is a wheel with a handle. A crane's crank is attached to a rope or line. When you turn the crank, the rope wraps around it, and the rest of the rope is pulled toward it.

PEOPLE HAVE USED CRANES for thousands of years to build monuments, temples, castles, and all sorts of things.

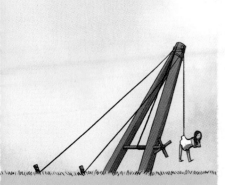

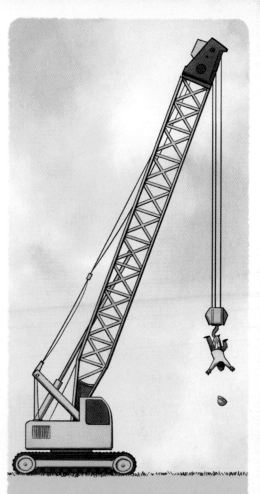

400-500 BCE

The first cranes were very simple: two wood poles tied together, with a pulley at the top and a hand crank at the bottom.

100s CE

Some ancient Roman cranes connected the crank to a giant wheel. People would turn the crank by walking inside the wheel!

1800s CE

In the 1800s, a variety of new cranes were invented that used coal, oil, or electricity to turn their cranks. New steel construction made it possible to build bigger, stronger cranes than ever before.

2000s CE

Today, most cranes use motors that are powered by electricity or gas to turn their cranks. Some modern cranes are so big that they have to be moved in parts and put together at the construction site.

ELEPHANTS CAN FLY!
The world's strongest crane, in China, could lift 3,000 elephants at once!

IT'S A DUMP TRUCK!

IT'S FOR DUMPING THINGS!

The truck has a PUMP that pushes LIQUID a little bit at a time into a TUBE beneath its bucket. As the liquid moves, it forces the front of the bucket up until everything inside falls out the back.

TREATS

BUCKET

LIQUID

PUMP

TUBE

TANK

FOOD

HOW CAN LIQUID PUSH THINGS?

Using liquid to push things is called **HYDRAULICS**.

Imagine two **CYLINDERS** in a pipe, with liquid between them.

When you push one of the cylinders, it pushes the liquid, and the liquid pushes the other cylinder.

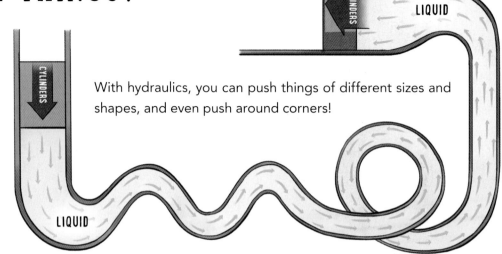

With hydraulics, you can push things of different sizes and shapes, and even push around corners!

THE FIRST DUMP TRUCK was invented in the 1880s, but it didn't use hydraulics to lift the front. Instead, it used a lever to lower the back.

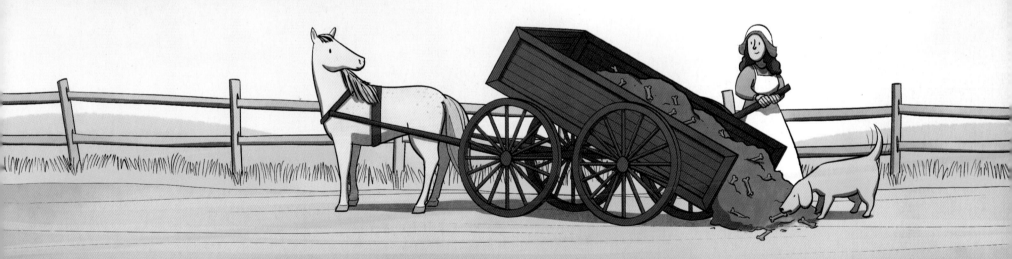

DINO MIGHT!

Some dump trucks can carry 50,000 pounds. That's almost as much as three *T. rexes*!

IT'S A TOILET!

IT'S FOR FLUSHING THINGS AWAY!

A toilet uses WATER to pull waste from a toilet bowl into sewage pipes. When you turn the HANDLE on the water tank behind the toilet, it LIFTS the tank's PLUG, and water flows into the bowl. Then the water drains through a hole and into a pipe, pulling everything else down with it.

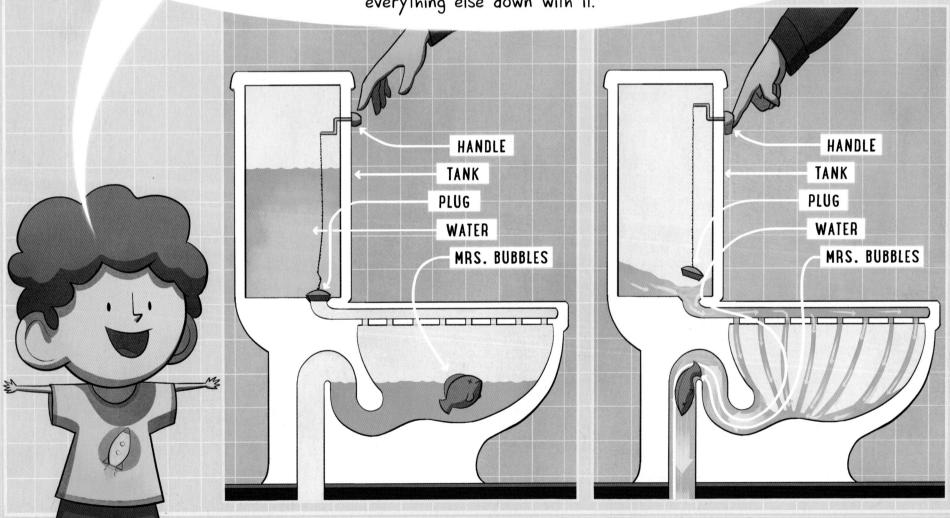

HANDLE

TANK

PLUG

WATER

MRS. BUBBLES

HANDLE

TANK

PLUG

WATER

MRS. BUBBLES

ANCIENT TOILETS

Thousands of years ago, most "toilets" were just holes in the ground. Some of the greatest ancient cities, like Mohenjo Daro in India, built their holes over flowing water.

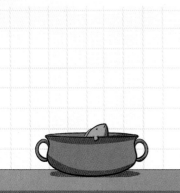

500s BCE

The most common ancient toilet was a chamber pot, which is just a bowl. You'd use one at night and dump it outside in the morning.

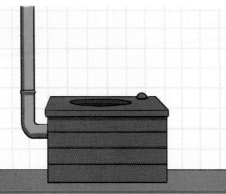

1590s CE

One of the first flushing toilets had its water tank upstairs, on the floor above the toilet. Letting the water down would flush everything out into a chamber beneath it. You'd have to clean out that chamber later and refill the water tank with buckets from a well.

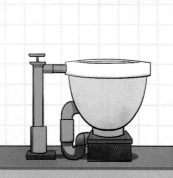

1770s CE

Later toilets included an S-shaped pipe beneath the bowl. The pipe kept some water in it between flushes, which blocked bad smells from wafting up from below.

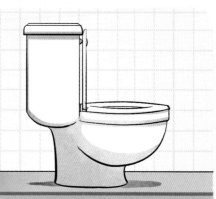

2000s CE

In the 1800s and 1900s, many towns and cities built pipes to bring running water to houses for the first time. Now after you flush, toilet tanks connected to water pipes can refill themselves!

POTTY TIME!

If you're like most people, you'll spend three months of your life using the toilet.

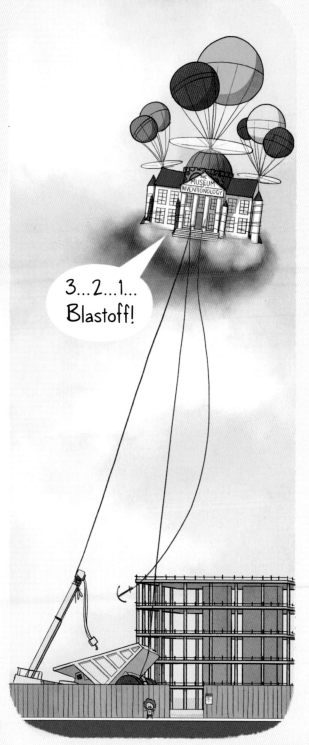

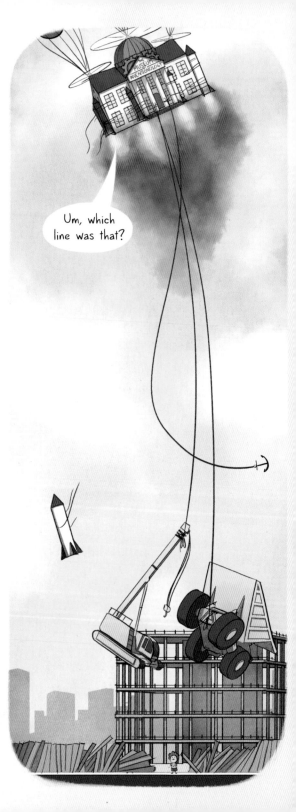

AUTHOR'S NOTE

This is a work of informational fiction. Anything that you learn from our child character is accurate. But beware the wacky Invention Hunters— almost nothing they say or do is wise, correct, or even possible!

Some concepts, dates, and diagrams have been generalized and simplified for ease of sharing and communicating to children. Where possible, illustrations are based on historical images, but in some cases where no visual record could be found, reasonable artistic license may have been used.

Special thanks to Elizabeth Segal for checking the facts and Delia Meza for providing an educational perspective during the book's development.

PORCELAIN THRONE
The watery marvel of ancient kings. Bestows majesty to those who sit upon it, and adds flavor to any drink sipped from it.

LITTER BOX
If you know where to find a cat large enough to use this luxurious waste collection device, please contact the front desk.

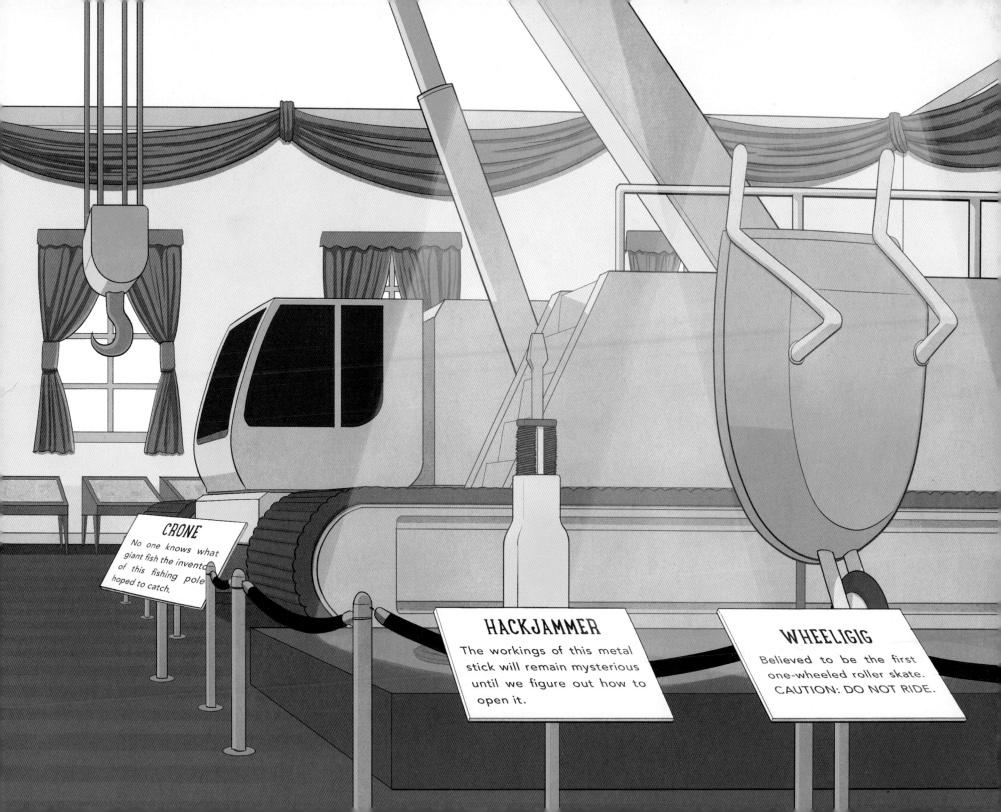

CRONE
No one knows what giant fish the invento̶r̶ of this fishing pole hoped to catch.

HACKJAMMER
The workings of this metal stick will remain mysterious until we figure out how to open it.

WHEELIGIG
Believed to be the first one-wheeled roller skate. CAUTION: DO NOT RIDE.

Photo © by Phoebe Ma

KORWIN BRIGGS is a writer and illustrator who makes books, comics, and infographics about history and science. He has written the Invention Hunters series, which includes *The Invention Hunters Discover How Machines Work*, *The Invention Hunters Discover How Electricity Works*, *The Invention Hunters Discover How Light Works*, and *The Invention Hunters Discover How Sound Works*. He's also the author and illustrator of *Gods and Heroes: Mythology Around the World* and a webcomic, *Veritable Hokum*. He lives in New York, and he invites you to visit his website at korwinbriggs.com.